Ooo-cha!

story by Colleen Sydor
art by Ruth Ohi

Annick Press Ltd.
Toronto • New York • Vancouver

We acknowledge the support of the Canada Council for the Arts for our
publishing program. We also thank the Ontario Arts Council.

We acknowledge the financial support of the Government of Canada through the
Book Publishing Industry Development Program for our publishing activities.

Cataloguing in Publication Data
Sydor, Colleen
    Ooo-cha!

ISBN 1-55037-605-5 (bound)   ISBN 1-55037-604-7 (pbk.)

I. Ohi, Ruth. II. Title.

PS8587.Y36O56 1999   jC813'.54   C99-930657-X
PZ7.S98275Oo 1999

The art in this book was rendered in watercolor, gouache, and pen and ink.
The text was typeset in Caslon 224.

Distributed in Canada by: Published in the U.S.A. by Annick Press (U.S.) Ltd.
Firefly Books Ltd.   Distributed in the U.S.A. by:
3680 Victoria Park Avenue   Firefly Books (U.S.) Inc.
Willowdale, ON   P.O. Box 1338
M2H 3K1   Ellicott Station
                                   Buffalo, NY 14205

Printed and bound in Canada by
Friesens, Altona, Manitoba.

For Bob and the chili peppers —
Brendan, Emily, Mahrie, Natascha and Porscha

nce there was a fearless young girl named Emily. One day her mother filled a basket with a gazillion goodies and told Emily to take them to her Great Granny Fanny, who lived at the other end of the Wild, Wild Forest.

"Emily," said her mother, "always remember your manners, and whatever you do, don't forget the magic word. Do you have your good witch wand with you?"

"Of course," said Emily, skipping off into the Wild, Wild Forest. "Don't worry, Mother, it'll be a piece of cake!"

Not long after she set out, Emily heard the snapping of twigs and the cracking of branches, and what should come jumping out at her from the Wild, Wild Forest but a wild, wild tiger.

"Young lady!" roared the tiger, "my nose tells me that you have in your basket a seven-layer chocolate cake with triple fudge icing. Seven-layer chocolate cake with triple fudge icing is my favorite, and if you don't hand it over, there will be trouble!"

"Why should I give you my Great Granny Fanny's chocolate cake?" asked Emily.

"Because," said the tiger, "I have teeth as big as daggers and claws as sharp as razors, and that should be reason enough!"

ou may have teeth as big as daggers and claws as sharp as razors," said Emily, "but you certainly don't have any manners, so you can have *this* instead." And she thunked the tiger over the head with her good witch wand and said the magic word,

"Ooo-cha!"

Instantly the tiger vanished, and in her place stood a beautiful tiger lily. Emily plucked the tiger lily and off she skipped, whistling and singing, and smelling her lovely flower.

oon Emily once again heard the snapping of twigs and cracking of branches, and what should come jumping out at her from the Wild, Wild Forest but a wild, wild dragon.

"Young lady!" bellowed the dragon, "my nose tells me that you have coconut-covered cherry rum balls in your basket. Coconut-covered cherry rum balls are my favorite. Hand them over or there will be trouble."

"Why should I give you Great Granny Fanny's cherry rum balls?" asked Emily.

"Because," said the dragon, "I can breathe fire and you cannot, and that should be reason enough!"

 may not be able to breathe fire," said Emily, "but at least I have good manners, and I also have *this*!" And she thunked the dragon in the belly with her good witch wand and said the magic word,

"Ooo-cha!"

Instantly the dragon disappeared, and in his place stood an elegant snapdragon. Emily plucked the snapdragon and off she skipped, whistling and singing, and smelling her lovely flowers.

mily wasn't the least bit surprised when, minutes later, a wild, wild bull jumped out of the Wild, Wild Forest and asked if he might please have a piece of her angel food cake with devil's delight frosting. Emily was thrilled.

"Finally!" she said, "a beast with some manners!" And she gave the bull a piece of cake. He didn't say "thank you," however, so Emily turned him into a bulrush and added it to her bouquet.

And so it went all afternoon, with Emily thunking ill-mannered beasts left and right. Among others, she added to her bouquet a dandelion (the lion had been far too greedy for his own good), a hollyhock (the hawk had never even *heard* of the word "please"), and a cowslip (the cow ate noisily, with her mouth open).

By the time a mere unsuspecting frog crossed her path, Emily had had enough. "Croak," said the frog. Emily was about to turn him into a crocus, but then she had a better idea. "What the heck," she said, and she picked him up and kissed him.

KABLAM! The frog disappeared, and in his place stood a scruffy old man with a rusty sword and a torn suit of armor. Emily was a little surprised.

"Why do you look so scruffy?" she asked.

"You would too if you'd been out of work for as long as I have," he said.

"What do you do?" asked Emily.

"I'm a dragon slayer," sighed the old man, "but I haven't seen a dragon in years."

"I may be able to help," said Emily. She gave the dragon slayer her snapdragon, stepped back, and said the magic word. But this time she said it backward!

"Aaaa-choo!"

Instantly the spell reversed itself. The flower
disappeared, and in its place stood the dragon.
The dragon slayer's face lit up. For a moment
he looked young again. He raised his sword high!

The dragon swallowed hard. Then he
turned around and ran for the hills. The
dragon slayer followed close behind with
a whoop and a holler.

mily skipped on merrily, and soon Great Granny Fanny's cottage came into sight. Just before going through the gate Emily opened the goody basket and slipped two pieces of seven-layer chocolate cake with triple fudge icing, two coconut-covered cherry rum balls, and two slices of angel food cake with devil's delight frosting into the pockets of her apron. Then she took the cowslip from her bouquet, tucked it into her hair, and rang the doorbell.

Someone opened the door, but it wasn't Great Granny Fanny! Instead, the cottage door swung slowly open and there stood ...

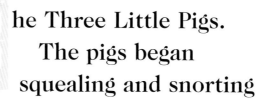he Three Little Pigs.
The pigs began
squealing and snorting
and falling all over each other in
their excitement. "Hand over the
basket!" they said, "or Granny will
pay!"

Emily could see Great Granny
Fanny neatly tied up in the corner,
but she had a twinkle in her eye.
Emily was not alarmed. She handed
the three greedy animals the basket
and they attacked it immediately,
making absolute pigs of themselves.

xcuse me," said Emily, "I thought you might also like these." And she tickled the pigs' noses with her wildflowers.

"Aaaa-choo!"

they squealed,

"Aaaa-choo! Aaaa-choo! Aaaa-choo!!!"

Suddenly it became very crowded in Granny Fanny's little cottage. The hungry beasts looked around drooling, and what was the first thing they saw? Three chocolate-covered pigs! Now if there's one thing a beast loves more than goodies, it's a pig *covered* in goodies. Supper and dessert all in one!

The three pigs swallowed hard, turned around, and ran out the door as fast as their legs would carry them. The beasts followed close behind, nipping at their curly little tails.

mily untied Great Granny Fanny and took the slightly squishy cakes from her pockets. Granny Fanny got out the good china. She put on the tea kettle.

"Heavens to Betsy!" she said, peering into the refrigerator. "All these goodies and not a drop of milk in the house!" Emily took the cowslip from her hair and waved it in front of Granny.

"Emily," said Granny, "you think of everything!"

hen they sat down and ate the goodies with their very best table manners. Emily even offered her coconut-covered cherry rum ball to the cow. (This time the cow had the good sense to eat with her mouth CLOSED!)